Rockets
STAN THE DOG

Stan and the
Crafty Cats

Ouch!

SCRIT!

Scou...on

For Emily

Rockets series:
CROOK CATCHERS - Karen Wallace & Judy Brown
HAUNTED MOUSE - Dee Shulman
LITTLE T - Frank Rodgers
MOTLEY'S CREW - Margaret Ryan & Margaret Chamberlain
MR CROC - Frank Rodgers
MRS MAGIC - Wendy Smith
MY FUNNY FAMILY - Colin West
ROVER - Chris Powling & Scoular Anderson
SILLY SAUSAGE - Michaela Morgan & Dee Shulman
SPACE TWINS - Wendy Smith
STAN THE DOG - Scoular Anderson
WIZARD'S BOY - Scoular Anderson

First paperback edition 2003
First published 2002 by A & C Black Publishers Ltd
37 Soho Square, London W1D 3QZ
www.acblack.com

Text and illustrations copyright © 2002 Scoular Anderson

The right of Scoular Anderson to be identified as author
and illustrator of this work has been asserted by him
in accordance with the Copyright, Designs and Patents Act 1988.

ISBN 0-7136-6139-9

A CIP catalogue record for this book is available
from the British Library.

A & C Black uses paper produced with elemental
chlorine-free pulp, harvested from managed sustainable forests.

Printed and bound by G. Z. Printek, Bilbao, Spain.

First Helping

Eating was the thing Stan liked doing best.

He also liked lying around.

He went to check out the gas fire in the sitting room. It wasn't on.

Another favourite sleeping place was near the radiator in the hall of his family's house. Just then the one Stan called Bigbelly started to vacuum.

The family's beds were really comfortable places to lie around. Stan wasn't supposed to jump on beds but he sneaked upstairs all the same.

When he got upstairs, Canopener was
already there, dusting.

Crumble and Handout were tidying their rooms.

Even Stan was tidied up. He was given a nice new collar.

He was so pleased with the collar he just had to go and find a mirror. He dashed to the bathroom and climbed up on a stool.
He admired himself from all sides.

Just then, he heard a familiar noise.

He ran back down to the kitchen.
Canopener had opened a can and made
lunch.

Then the family sat down for lunch, too.
Stan usually sat under the table waiting
for Crumble to drop crumbs or Handout
to give him a handout. But not today.

Stan was right. After lunch, the family rushed around putting on jackets.

Stan wasn't going, though.

The front door slammed. The car doors slammed. The car drove off. Stan had a wonderful thought.

Crumble is having a friend to stay!

That will mean two lots of crumbs...

...two lots of dropped crisps...

...two lots of chocolate!

Stan could hardly believe his luck.

Second Helping

Some time later, Stan heard the car coming into the drive. He dashed to the front door.

The family came in, one by one. Canopener and Bigbelly...

...then Handout and Crumble...

...then a very large lady.

The front door was shut.

Stan dashed through to the sitting room
and climbed up on a chair.

Out in the car, two pairs of eyes stared
back at him.

Stan went back into the kitchen and learned the truth.

Bigbelly and
Handout went
out to the car
and brought
in two baskets.

Clementine was in one of them.

SPUT!

Charming!

Clifford was in the other.

Ouch!

SCRIT!

Largelady opened the baskets and took
out the cats.

Stan was less than pleased.

Largelady put the cats down.

Clifford and Clementine began to look around.

Third Helping

The trouble started quite soon. Stan was lying beside the hall radiator minding his own business when the cats came to stare at him.

They give me the creeps.

Stan couldn't stand it any more so he got up and left.

Huh!

He went upstairs.

He had just settled himself on Crumble's bed when he was aware of two pairs of eyes staring at him.

He gave up Crumble's bed to the cats and went off to Handout's room. However, the real trouble started at tea-time. Stan bounded downstairs when he heard the sound of cans being opened.

He rushed into the kitchen to find
Clifford eating *his* dinner.

As he ran forward, Clementine suddenly
dived out of a cupboard.

Stan was not
amused.

As the cats had been eating *his* food, Stan decided he would eat *theirs*. He made a dash for their dishes...

...but Clifford and Clementine ran under his feet...

...and sent him flying.

Stan ended up with a foot in each dish...

...and the cat food ended up all over the kitchen. Stan was in the dog house.

Fourth Helping

The next day was even worse. Stan found it very hard to ignore the cats. They seemed to be everywhere. They stole his place under the table at breakfast time.

Peace at last.

The peace and quiet didn't last long.

Largelady and Crumble brought the cats out into the garden, too. They were going to have their daily brush.

After the brushing, Largelady tied ribbons round the cats' necks.

That gave Crumble an idea. She rushed
into the house and came back with an
armful of clothes.

Crumble put a hat on Stan's head.

She managed to get him into a nightie.

Then she tied a big ribbon round his neck.

She dashed into the garden shed...

...and came out with her old pushchair.

You must be joking!

Stan was bundled into the pushchair even though he put up a fight.

Now, let's all go for a walk!

Largelady put leads on the cats.

They went out of the back gate and into the lane. Crumble was having great fun.

She was jumping about so much that she tripped and let go of the pushchair...

...and off it went, down the hill.

Stan couldn't get out of the pushchair
until he hit a big pile of rubbish at the
bottom of the lane.

Stan's horror wasn't over yet.

Stan got
the blame
once again...

...and he was dragged off home to have
a bath.

Just to make matters worse, he had lost
his lovely new collar down by the canal.

Fifth Helping

That evening, Clementine and Clifford disappeared. Largelady was in such a state.

The family came to see what was happening.

Crumble and Handout searched upstairs.

Canopener searched downstairs.

Bigbelly searched the garden.

Largelady sat and cried but the cats were nowhere to be found.

After that, the family went to bed. The house was very quiet.

But Stan couldn't sleep.

Stan got out of his bed.

He stretched up
and unlocked
the back door.

He went down the back garden.

He went out
of the back
gate and into
the lane.

He went down the lane towards the canal.
The lane was filled with nighttime noises.

Rats scattered in every direction as he reached the canal.

He caught sight of them at last. They were running around near the big pile of rubbish he had fallen into that afternoon.

Stan walked back to the rubbish heap. The two cats were rushing around as if they were looking for something.

The cats began to run back in the direction of the house.

Then they leapt onto a fence beside the canal.

But just as they did so, they were scared
by a passing owl...

...and they
tumbled
into the
canal below.

Stan ran up and peered into the dark
water. There was nothing to be seen...

...until a bubble burst on the surface.

Stan knew he had to get the cats out before they drowned. He nosed about in the water until he found something.

At last he touched something that moved.

It was
Clementine.

He pulled
Clifford out, too.

The cats were
covered in weed
and mud and
slime.

Stan dumped them in Crumble's old
pushchair which was still sitting by
the pile of rubbish.

He pushed the cats back up the lane.

He took them into the house and up to
the bathroom. He turned on the shower.

Stan lifted them out of the shower and onto a towel.

At that moment, he saw that Clementine was holding something tightly in her mouth.

Just then, all the bedroom doors opened.
Everyone had come to see what the
noise was.

Largelady was overjoyed.

At the end of the week, Largelady was taken to the station.

Stan could lie around anywhere he wanted. Crumble was his friend again and let him lie on her bed.